SPACE TRAVEL

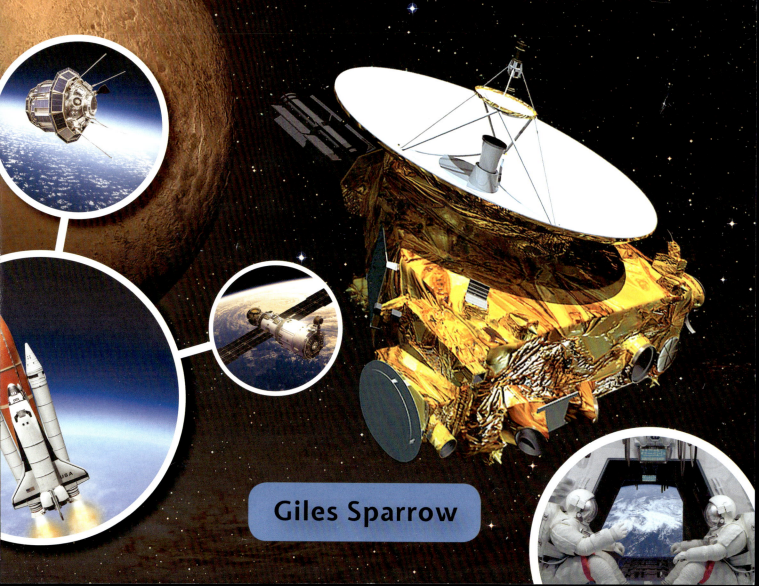

Giles Sparrow

Published in 2018 by Enslow Publishing, LLC.
101 W. 23rd Street, Suite 240, New York, NY 10011

Library of Congress Cataloging-in-Publication Data

Names: Sparrow, Giles, 1970- author.
Title: Space travel / Giles Sparrow.
Description: New York, NY : Enslow Publishing, 2018. | Series: Space explorers | Audience: K to Grade 4. | Includes bibliographical references and index.
Identifiers: LCCN 2017031493| ISBN 9780766092686 (library bound) | ISBN 9780766094017 (pbk.) | ISBN 9780766094024 (6 pack)
Subjects: LCSH: Manned space flight—Juvenile literature. | Space tourism—Juvenile literature.
Classification: LCC TL793 .S68885 2018 | DDC 629.45—dc23
LC record available at https://lccn.loc.gov/2017031493

Printed in the United States of America

To Our Readers: We have done our best to make sure all websites in this book were active and appropriate when we went to press. However, the author and the publisher have no control over and assume no liability for the material available on those websites or on any websites they may link to. Any comments or suggestions can be sent by e-mail to customerservice@enslow.com.

Picture Credits:
Key: b-bottom, t-top, c-center, l-left, r-right Alamy: 8-9 (Photo Researchers, Inc); ESA: 20-21 (D. Ducros); EUMETSAT: 20b; Getty Images: 9tr (NASA/Apollo/Science Faction), 9cl (Sovfoto), 21b (Detlef van Ravenswaay), 24-25 (Stefan Morrell); NASA: 13tr (JSC), 14-15 (Bill Stafford/JSC), 14br & 26br (Mark Sowa/JSC), 15bl, 16tr & 27tl, 18br & 27tr, 19tr, 21r & 27cl & 30b, 22-23 (JPL-Caltech), 22c (JPL/ Space Science Institute), 23r & 27br (JHU APL/SwRI/Steve Gribben), 24br (JPL-Caltech/SETI Institute), 28br, 29tr 29bl; Shutterstock: cover & title page main (muratart), tl (Andrey Armyagov), bl (siraphat), c (3Dsculptor), br (iurii), 4-5 (Stefano Garau), 4cl (MaraQu), 4b (Viktar Malyshchyts), 4cr (NASA), 5t & 31tr (tose), 5br & 30t (pixbox77), 6-7 (3Dsculptor), 6c (Fred Mantel), 6br & 26tr (stoyanh), 7tr (Georgios Kollidas), 9br (Bon Appetit), 10-11 & 10br & 11tr & 26cr (Everett Historical), 11br (stoyanh), 12-13 (vicspacewalker), 13cr (Christopher Halloran), 13br & 26bl (Andrew Rybalko), 16-17 (Stefan Ataman), 16-17 b/g (Viktar Malyshchyts), 16bl (Bannykh Alexey Vladimirovich), 16cr (Pavel L Photo and Video), 18-19 (Naeblys/NASA), 18bl & 19br (PavloArt Studio), 20c (Johan Swanepoel), 22bl (MawRhis), 25br (Sebastian Kaulitzki), 26tl (Kiev.Victor), 27bl (Vadim Sadovski), 28tl & 31b (Vadim Sadovski); Wikimedia Commons: 25tl (SpaceX).

Enslow Publishing
101 W. 23rd Street
Suite 240
New York, NY 10011
USA
enslow.com

CONTENTS

Introduction

Our Universe is a huge area of space made up of everything we can see in every direction. It contains a great number of different objects—from tiny specks of cosmic dust to mighty galaxy superclusters. The most interesting of these are planets, stars and nebulae, galaxies, and clusters of galaxies.

Stars

A star is a dense (tightly packed) ball of gas that shines through chemical reactions in its core (middle). Our Sun is a star. Stars range from red dwarfs, much smaller and fainter than the Sun, to supergiants a hundred times larger and a million times brighter.

Planets

A planet is a large ball of rock or gas that orbits (travels around) a star. In our solar system there are eight "major" planets, several dwarf planets, and countless smaller objects. These range from asteroids and comets down to tiny specks of dust.

Nebulae

The space between the stars is filled with mostly unseen clouds of gas and dust called nebulae. Where they collapse (fall in) and grow dense enough to form new stars, they light up from within.

Galaxies

A galaxy is a huge cloud of stars, gas, and dust, including nebulae, held together by a force called gravity. There are many different types of galaxy. This is because their shape, the nature of their stars, and the amount of gas and dust within them can vary.

This is our home galaxy, the Milky Way, seen from Earth. Our view of the Universe depends on what we can see using the best technologies that we have.

Galaxy Clusters

Gravity makes galaxies bunch together to form clusters that are millions of light-years wide. These clusters join together at the edges to form even bigger superclusters—the largest structures in the Universe.

Rockets

Rising into space on a jet of flames, rockets need an explosive chemical reaction to push them through Earth's atmosphere. They are noisy, wasteful, and expensive, but they are still the best way of reaching orbit around the Earth.

A rocket stage is mostly made of fuel tanks and engines. Only a small cargo on the top reaches space.

Stage by Stage

Most rockets are made up of many "stages," each with their own fuel tanks and rocket engines. These stages may be stacked on top of each other, or sit side by side. Only the top stage reaches orbit with its cargo—the burnt-out lower stages fall back to Earth and are usually destroyed.

Booster stages help to raise the speed of the top stage and cargo before falling back to Earth.

NASA's Space Launch System will carry the *Orion* spacecraft into orbit.

The *V–2* was a rocket with explosive cargo, used as a weapon during World War II. Most modern rockets are based on the *V–2*.

SPACECRAFT PROFILE

Name: *Saturn V*
Launch dates: 1967-73
Total launches: 13
Height: 363 ft (110.6 m)
Diameter: 33 ft (10.1 m)
Weight: 5.04 million lb
(2.29 million kg)

Action and Reaction

Rockets rely on a rule that the English scientist Isaac Newton worked out in 1687: "For every action, there is an equal and opposite reaction." This means that the force of exploding gases coming from a rocket engine is always the same as the reaction: The force pushing the engine itself in the opposite direction. The rocket pushes against itself, not the air around it, so it can work even in space, where there is no air.

First stage with four rocket engines.

Isaac Newton discovered the principle of the rocket.

Pioneers

The first satellites and astronauts were launched during the "space race," a time of competition between the United States and Russia. Both sides made huge breakthroughs while they each tried to beat the other country and complete many space "firsts."

Russian astronaut Yuri Gagarin became the first man in space during the *Vostok 1* mission on April 12, 1961.

Race to the Moon

The Soviet Union (a group of with Russia) put the first satellite in space in 1957, and the first man in space four years later. The United States found it hard to catch up. It ended up winning the space race thanks to its Apollo missions, which landed the first astronauts on the Moon in July 1969.

American astronaut Neil Armstrong was the first person to step onto the Moon.

Laika's Story

After the successful launch of the *Sputnik 1* satellite in October 1957, Russian politicians ordered their engineers to work on a new "spectacular." The answer was *Sputnik 2*, a much larger satellite that carried a living passenger—Laika. This small dog had been picked up as a stray and specially trained. Sadly, Laika died from stress shortly after launch.

Laika was the first animal to orbit the Earth.

SPACECRAFT PROFILE

Name: *Vostok 1*
Launch date: April 12, 1961
Diameter: 7.5 ft (2.3 m)
Flight duration: 108 minutes
Orbits: 1
Launch site: Baikonur, now in Kazakhstan
Crew: Yuri Gagarin

The Space Shuttle

After the end of the space race, the U.S. space agency NASA started working on a new kind of spacecraft—a reusable spaceplane to make space travel more common. Although it completed some amazing missions, the space shuttle wasn't as useful or reliable as hoped, and it was retired in 2011.

Shuttle Launch

The space shuttle system was made up of a plane-like "orbiter" vehicle with a large cargo hold and rocket engines on its tail. It launched into orbit fuelled by a huge external (outside) tank, and helped out by two strap-on booster rockets. These boosters fell away during takeoff but could be found and reused.

The shuttle blasts off from Launch Complex 39 at NASA's Kennedy Space Center.

Gliding back to Earth

After finishing its mission, the shuttle orbiter dropped back into Earth's atmosphere in a fiery process called re-entry. When it was back in the atmosphere, the shuttle moved like a giant high-speed glider, heading for a landing strip in either California or Florida, U.S.A.. When it touched down at a speed of about 213 mph (343 km/h), the tail part released parachutes that helped the wheel brakes to stop the shuttle.

Black tiles on the underside of the shuttle were designed to shield it from the heat of re-entry. During a 2003 mission, some were damaged. As a result, upon reentry, the shuttle Columbia exploded.

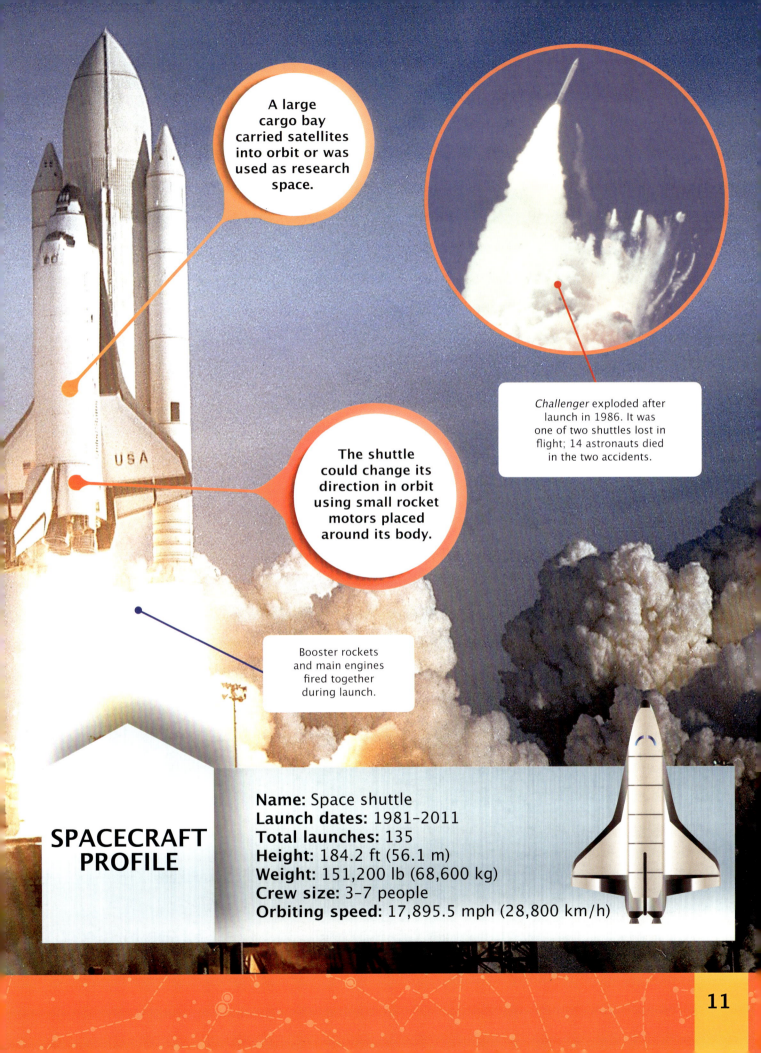

A large cargo bay carried satellites into orbit or was used as research space.

Challenger exploded after launch in 1986. It was one of two shuttles lost in flight; 14 astronauts died in the two accidents.

The shuttle could change its direction in orbit using small rocket motors placed around its body.

Booster rockets and main engines fired together during launch.

SPACECRAFT PROFILE

Name: Space shuttle
Launch dates: 1981–2011
Total launches: 135
Height: 184.2 ft (56.1 m)
Weight: 151,200 lb (68,600 kg)
Crew size: 3–7 people
Orbiting speed: 17,895.5 mph (28,800 km/h)

Launchpads

Sending rockets and their cargo into space is a dangerous and noisy business. Space agencies build large, specialized launch areas that are a long way from where people live.

Fuel is not pumped into the tanks until the rocket is in position on the launchpad.

At Baikonur, Kazakhstan, rockets are moved around on huge trains. They are only stood upright when they reach the launchpad.

Russia has used the *Soyuz* rocket since the 1960s.

Launch towers lock into place around the rocket and release during takeoff.

Escape rocket system pulls crew capsule away from the main rocket in an emergency.

Mission Controllers

Rocket launches are watched from a control room inside the launch area. Not long after the rocket has safely left the pad, control passes to a separate mission control room that may be far away. For example, NASA's mission control at Houston, Texas, is more than a thousand miles from its launchpads at Cape Canaveral, Florida.

Experts check different parts of the spacecraft's systems from their desks.

Sea Launch's command ship and launch platform.

Floating Launchpad

Sea Launch is a company that offers rocket launches from a floating platform called *Ocean Odyssey.* By placing the platform close to the equator in the Pacific Ocean, rockets can use the speed boost from the Earth's rotation. Missions are cheaper because they use less fuel and can carry heavier cargo. Launching at sea also means there is a smaller risk of rockets falling back on areas where there are people.

SPACECRAFT PROFILE

Name: *Soyuz* rocket
Launch dates: 1966–present
Total launches: 1,700+
Height: 162.4 ft (49.5 m) in current version
Weight: 672,000 lb (305,000 kg)

Astronaut Training

Only a few hundred people have gone into space until now, and most of them had years of training before their launch. Some astronauts are specialist pilots, and many are scientists or engineers.

In the Tank

Sometimes an astronaut will need to do difficult work while he or she is weightless and wearing a bulky spacesuit. The best way to train for this on Earth is in a special water tank. Astronauts wear a suit designed for training and use dummy tools for practice. Divers watch over them.

Space Tourists

Not all astronauts are professionals (trained experts). Since the 1990s, Russia has given wealthy space fans the chance to make short trips into orbit—if they can pay a few million dollars toward the costs of the *Soyuz* rocket. These space tourists still go through many months of training, however—if only to make sure they don't get in the way of the professionals!

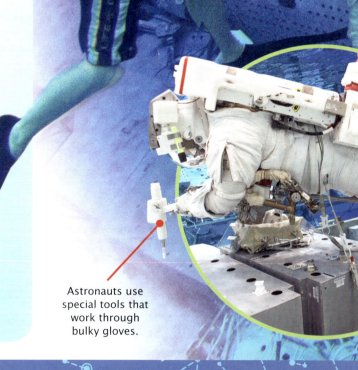

Astronauts use special tools that work through bulky gloves.

NASA's Neutral Buoyancy Laboratory at Houston, Texas, has one of the world's largest diving tanks.

An air bag helps to make sure the astronaut is floating without rising or sinking. This is called neutral buoyancy.

Dummy space station pieces are used to learn techniques for building in space.

English scientist Stephen Hawking flew on a reduced-gravity plane in 2007.

Floating or Falling?

Astronauts and others can enjoy feeling weightless for a short time by flying on a reduced-gravity aircraft. These planes fly up to great heights before diving at a speed that is the same as the pull of Earth's gravity. As people and objects on board fall at the same speed as the plane, they are in zero gravity for up to 25 seconds at a time.

Early Space Stations

The inside of *Mir* became cluttered and messy over the years.

A space station is a base that is in orbit around the Earth, where astronauts can live and work for weeks or even months. The first stations were launched by Russia and the United States in the 1970s, and Russia carried on building them and improving their designs for the next 20 years.

Record-Breakers

From 1971, Russia launched a series of seven stations called *Salyut*. NASA, meanwhile, launched a single station called *Skylab*, which was visited by three crews in 1973–74. In 1986, Russia began building *Mir*, an orbital laboratory with a few different modules (units) for living and working. Russian astronauts working on *Mir* set a number of records including the first person to spend a year in space.

A Russian *Soyuz* unit attached to *Mir* was used as a lifeboat by the crew in emergencies.

SPACECRAFT PROFILE

Name: *Skylab*
Launch date: May 14, 1973
Width: 55.8 ft (17 m)
Length: 82.4 ft (25.1 m)
Completed missions: 3
Crew size: 3 people per mission
Re-entry: July 11, 1979 (burnt up and crashed in Western Australia)

Together in Orbit

Beween 1995 and 1998, the U.S. space shuttles made a few visits to Russia's *Mir* space station. U.S. astronauts stayed on the station between missions, and the shuttle delivered goods and tools to *Mir*.

Mir was built out of seven units launched over ten years.

Each new module was fitted with its own solar panels for electrical power.

The space shuttle *Atlantis* was specially designed to dock with *Mir*.

The Kvant-2 module offered extra living space as the station's crew grew.

International Space Station

The *International Space Station* (ISS) is the ninth space station that humans have built in space. It is the first one where agencies from different countries have worked together—16 nations are part of the project. The *ISS* is the largest and most expensive spacecraft ever built.

Panel Power

The *ISS* has eight pairs of solar panels. Solar cells in the panels change energy from the Sun into electricity. A system of trusses (joining corridors) connects the different modules. They hold electrical lines, cooling lines for machines, and mobile transporter rails. The solar panels and robotic arms fix to the trusses, too.

The *ISS*'s solar panels can produce (make) up to 110 kW of power.

Zvezda docking port

Solar panel

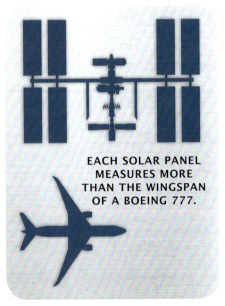

EACH SOLAR PANEL MEASURES MORE THAN THE WINGSPAN OF A BOEING 777.

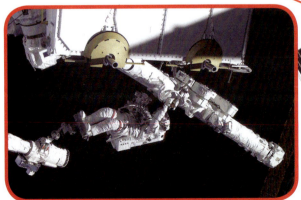

Life on the Station

The *ISS* has three laboratories: The Columbus laboratory, the Kibo laboratory, and the U.S. Destiny laboratory. Every day, *ISS* crew carry out science experiments in the labs, and scientists on Earth also take part. There are research projects into making new materials and growing special crystals.

Kibo laboratory

U.S. Destiny laboratory

Columbus laboratory

Canadarm 2

NASA astronaut Karen Nyberg at work in the U.S. Destiny laboratory.

The first *ISS* module launched into orbit was the Russian–built Zarya, in 1998.

SPACECRAFT PROFILE

Name: *International Space Station*
Launch date: 1998 (latest module, 2017)
Width: 358 ft (109 m)
Length: 289 ft (88 m)
Weight: 462.5 tons (419.6 tonnes)
Orbiting speed: 17,895.5 mph (8 km/s)
Crew size: 3–6 people

Satellites

Satellites are robot spacecraft put in orbit around Earth to do a many different jobs. Some watch the weather, or photograph our planet to learn more about it. Others help us communicate, or find our way around the world.

Different Orbits

Satellites are put into an orbit that is best for the job they have to do. Some sit happily in a Low Earth Orbit (LEO) that puts them just beyond the atmosphere. Others enter much higher geostationary (fixed) orbit above the equator, where they stay above a single point on Earth's surface. Satellites that try to study the whole of Earth's surface are put in tilted orbits that loop above and below the Earth's poles as the planet rotates beneath them.

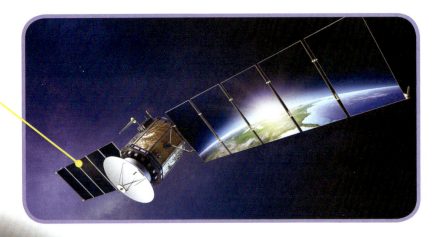

Communications satellites often use geostationary orbits.

Cameras take images of Europe and Africa every 15 minutes.

SPACECRAFT PROFILE

Name: *Meteosat 10*
Launch date: July 5, 2012
Diameter: 10.5 ft (3.2 m)
Height: 7.9 ft (2.4 m)
Orbit: 22,236 miles (35,786 km)
Orbital period: 23 h 56 m
(matching Earth's rotation)

Drum-shaped satellite spins 100 times per second.

Space Helpers

The curved shape of the Earth makes it impossible to send radio signals (which travel in straight lines) very far. Communication satellites solve this problem. Orbiting high above Earth, they can be seen from places on Earth that are far away from each other. This means signals can be bounced from one place to another along two straight-line paths.

The European-built *Meteosat* satellites are designed to watch weather on Earth from an orbit high above the equator.

NASA's Tracking and Data Relay satellites are designed for communication with orbiting spacecraft.

Sputnik 1 was the first satellite, launched in October 1957. Its 185-lb (84-kg) metal ball held a simple radio beacon that could send and receive signals.

Space Probes

Humans have not made it farther into space than the Moon, but we have still been able to explore much of the solar system using space probes. These robot explorers have now visited all the major planets and many smaller worlds, too.

Specialist Robots

Probes are designed to carry out one kind of mission. Some probes are orbiters that will become satellites of other planets. Others may carry out high-speed flyby missons and collect information as they fly past. Some probes are built to land on the surface of planets or moons, and even drive across their surface.

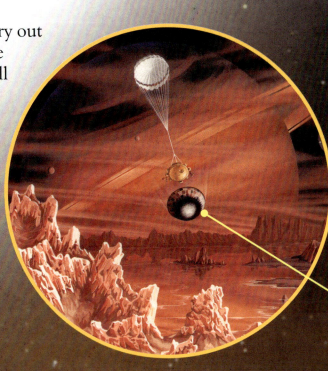

The *Huygens* lander was designed to parachute into the atmosphere of Saturn's moon, Titan.

SPACECRAFT PROFILE

Name: *Voyager 2*
Launch date: August 20, 1977
Weight: 1,820 lb (825.5 kg)
Electrical power: 470 W
Current speed: 34,000 mph (55,000 km/h)
Targets: Jupiter, Saturn, Uranus, and Neptune

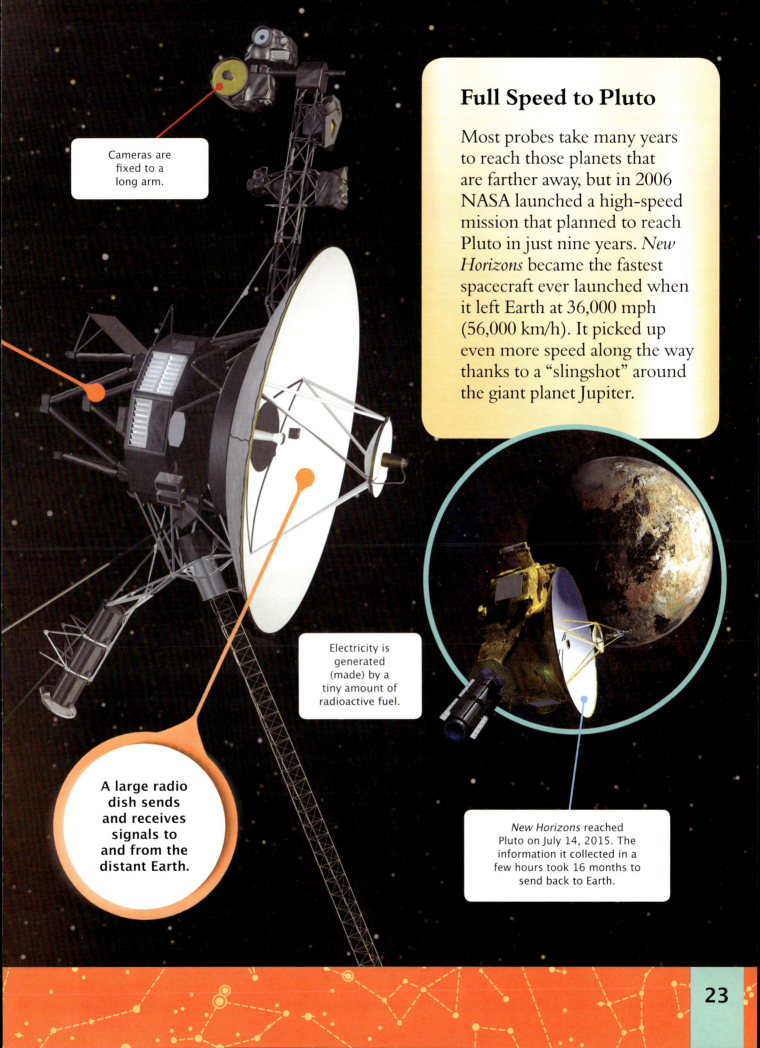

Cameras are fixed to a long arm.

Full Speed to Pluto

Most probes take many years to reach those planets that are farther away, but in 2006 NASA launched a high-speed mission that planned to reach Pluto in just nine years. *New Horizons* became the fastest spacecraft ever launched when it left Earth at 36,000 mph (56,000 km/h). It picked up even more speed along the way thanks to a "slingshot" around the giant planet Jupiter.

Electricity is generated (made) by a tiny amount of radioactive fuel.

A large radio dish sends and receives signals to and from the distant Earth.

New Horizons reached Pluto on July 14, 2015. The information it collected in a few hours took 16 months to send back to Earth.

The Future

Although astronauts have not journeyed farther than Earth's orbit since the early 1970s, space probes have flown much farther and changed our view of the solar system. In the next few years, however, we should finally begin a new age of space missions with crews on board.

Terraforming Mars

Mars has a lot more to offer than the Moon when it comes to creating new living spaces for humans on another world. The main problem is that it is a lot farther away. In the future, though, some scientists think we might be able to change the planet's climate and "terraform" it into a world much more like Earth.

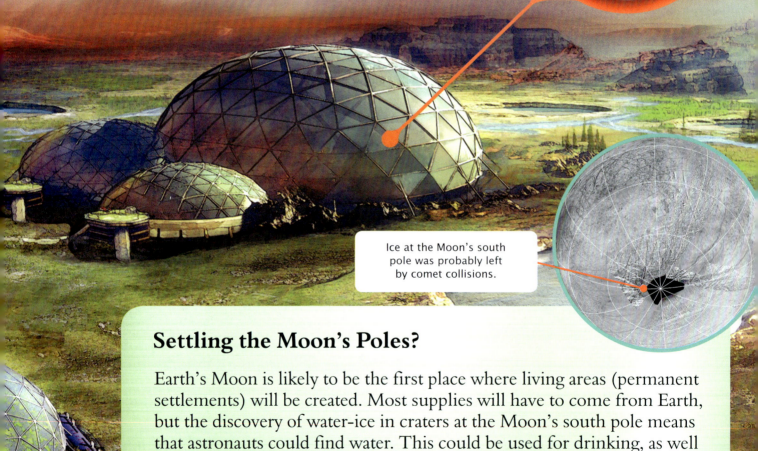

Living domes keep Earth-like air inside, protecting those inside from the thin, toxic Martian atmosphere.

Ice at the Moon's south pole was probably left by comet collisions.

Settling the Moon's Poles?

Earth's Moon is likely to be the first place where living areas (permanent settlements) will be created. Most supplies will have to come from Earth, but the discovery of water-ice in craters at the Moon's south pole means that astronauts could find water. This could be used for drinking, as well as for generating (making) power and air that humans can breathe.

SPACECRAFT PROFILE

Name: *Interplanetary Transport System*
Company: SpaceX
Launch date: 2020s (planned)
Height: 400 ft (122 m)
Weight: 23.1 million lb (10.5 million kg)
Payload: 990,000 lb (450,000 kg) to Mars with refuelling in Earth orbit

As the air thickens, small aircraft can be used for transport.

SpaceX's rocket could land a hundred people, or a huge amount of equipment, on Mars, helping to build up the first cities.

Part of terraforming is creating a way to trap heat from the Sun, so the planet never gets too cold.

Over the centuries, water would melt out of the Martian surface. Plants could spread long before humans and animals could step outside without protection.

Hardy Earth micro-animals such as this tardigrade (water bear) can survive in lots of environments. They may be able to live on Mars even today.

Did You Know?

There's always more to learn about what lies in the vastness of space. Boost your knowledge with these amazing facts about space travel.

The *Saturn V* rocket that took astronauts to the Moon in 1969 is still the **biggest rocket** ever built.

The first woman in space, **Valentina Tereshkova**, flew on *Vostok 6* in June 1963.

There were five working **space shuttles** in total (*Columbia*, *Challenger*, *Discovery*, *Atlantis*, and *Endeavour*), plus a prototype called *Enterprise*.

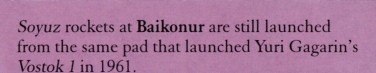

Soyuz rockets at **Baikonur** are still launched from the same pad that launched Yuri Gagarin's *Vostok 1* in 1961.

The **Neutral Buoyancy Laboratory** pool holds 6.2 million gallons (23,500 kl) of water.

In 1997, a **supply spacecraft** without crew on board crashed into *Mir*, creating damage that almost forced the crew to leave the station.

Canadarm 2, the *ISS*'s main robotic arm, is 55 ft (16.7 m) long and can lift weights up to 127.8 tons (116 tonnes).

The **higher** a satellite orbits, the longer it takes to go around Earth.

Five space probes followed paths that sent them out of our solar system altogether. Each holds a **message** from Earth for any aliens that may find it.

Gravity on Mars is just **40%** of Earth's, so the muscles of people who move to Mars may be too weak to cope back on their home planet.

Your Questions Answered

Scientists now know an incredible amount about space travel, but space is still bursting with amazing information; there are always more questions to be answered. This is what makes people want to become scientists and astronauts, and to study space. Here are the answers to some interesting questions about space, then you can start asking more!

How can I become an astronaut?

It's a long road so the first thing you'll need is determination, and after that, a lot of hard work.

To apply for a space program with NASA or the ESA, you need to have a good degree—in science, engineering, or math—and be in tip-top physical condition. Added to this you will need experience; for example, pilots will need 1,000 hours in a fast jet. Alongside this, is the ability to stay calm in emergency situations.

How much does it cost to go into space?

It cost approximately $450 million per mission to launch the Space Shuttle. NASA's latest rocket, the Space Launch System, is set to be completed in 2018 and will launch the *Orion* spacecraft. Each launch will cost approximately $500 million.

Several companies are now offering ordinary people the chance to take a trip into space—though they would have to go through a lot of training. Tickets are a costly $250,000! You would take off in a jet and climb to over 50,000 ft (15,000 m) above Earth, where a rocket would then boost you into Earth's orbit. All aboard would experience weightlessness and get a good view of Earth from space. Time in space would last just a few minutes before passengers return to their seats and prepare for re-entry.

How was the *International Space Station* built?

The answer is, a little bit at a time. The *ISS* is approximately the size of a football field, so it would be impossible to launch it in one go from the Earth. Building began in 1998 and took more than 40 separate missions. All the separate pieces of the Space Station were taken into orbit, where it was put together.

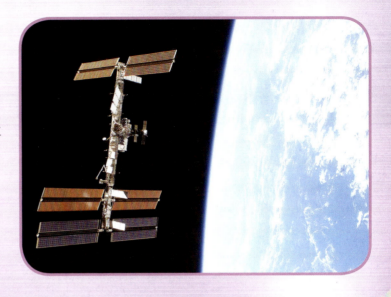

How do rockets engines work?

Rockets carry fuel in big containers. Within the engine, a chemical reaction is started and a hot gas produced. This gas is let out of the back of the engine and it pushes out with such force that it pushes the rocket forward.

What fuel do rockets use?

Some rockets, such as the Russian *Soyuz* rocket, use liquid fuel. Others, such as the side boosters on the Space Shuttle, use solid fuel. The type of fuel chosen depends on the job that the rocket needs to do. Solid fuels are usually made of two chemicals in a powder form that are mixed together and then compressed into a solid "cake." Solid fuels burn continuously once ignited, so can be used only once. Liquid fuels, usually liquid hydrogen or liquid oxygen, can be used a little at a time.

Glossary

asteroid A small rocky object made up of material left over from the birth of the solar system.

atmosphere A shell of gases kept around a planet, star, or other object by its gravity.

comet A chunk of rock and ice from the edge of the solar system. Close to the Sun, its melting ices form a coma and a tail.

galaxy A large system of stars, gas, and dust with anything from millions to trillions of stars.

gravity A natural force created around objects with mass, which draws other objects toward them.

light-year The distance covered by light in a year—about 5.9 trillion miles (9.5 quadrillion km).

Milky Way Our home galaxy, a spiral with a bar across its core. Our solar system is about 28,000 light-years from the monster black hole at its heart.

Moon Earth's closest companion in space, a ball of rock that orbits Earth every 27.3 days. Most other planets in the solar system have moons of their own.

nebula A cloud of gas or dust floating in space. Nebulae are the raw material used to make stars.

orbit A fixed path taken by one object in space around another because of the effect of gravity.

planet A world that orbits the Sun, which has enough mass and gravity to pull itself into a ball-like shape, and clear space around it of other large objects.

red dwarf A small, faint star with a cool red surface and less than half the mass of the Sun.

red giant A huge, brilliant (very bright) star near the end of its life, with a cool, red surface. Red giants are stars that have used up the fuel supply in their core and are going through big changes in order to keep shining for a little longer.

rocket A vehicle that drives itself forward through a controlled chemical explosion and can therefore travel in the vacuum of space. Rockets are the only practical way to launch spacecraft and satellites.

satellite Any object orbiting a planet. Moons are natural satellites made of rock and ice. Artificial (manmade) satellites are machines in orbit around Earth.

space probe A robot vehicle that explores the solar system and sends back signals to Earth.

spacecraft A vehicle that travels into space.

telescope A device that collects light or other radiations from space and uses them to create a bright, clear image. Telescopes can use either a lens or a mirror to collect light.

Further Information

BOOKS

Daynes, Katie. *See Inside Space*. London, UK: Usborne Publishing, 2008.

DK Reference. *Space!* New York, NY: DK Publishing, 2015.

Kelly, Scott. *My Journey to the Stars*. New York, NY: Crown Books for Young Readers, 2017.

Murphy, Glenn. *Space: The Whole Whizz-Bang Story* (Science Sorted). New York, NY: Macmillan Children's Books, 2013.

Newman, Ben. *Professor Astro Cat's Frontiers of Space*. London, UK: Flying Eye Books, 2013.

Rogers, Simon. *Information Graphics: Space*. Somerville, MA: Big Picture Press, 2015.

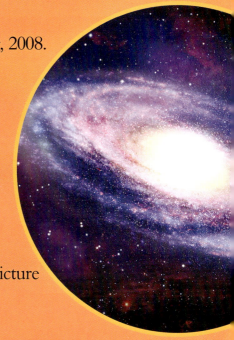

WEBSITES

www.nasa.gov/kidsclub/index.html
Join Nebula at NASA Kids' Club to play games and learn about space.

www.ngkids.co.uk/science-and-nature/ten-facts-about-space
Get started with these ten great facts about space, then explore the rest of the National Geographic Kids site for more fun.

www.esa.int/esaKIDSen/
Explore this site from the European Space Agency. There's information, games, and news.

Index